The Books About Addy

Meet Addy · An American Girl

Addy and her mother try to escape from slavery because they hope to be free and to reunite their family.

❋

Addy Learns a Lesson · A School Story

Addy starts her life as a free person in Philadelphia. She learns about reading and writing—and freedom.

❋

Addy's Surprise · A Christmas Story

Addy and Momma are generous with the little money they've saved—and thrilled by a great surprise.

❋

Happy Birthday, Addy! · A Springtime Story

Addy makes a new friend, who encourages her to claim a birthday and helps her face prejudice.

❋

Addy Saves the Day · A Summer Story

The Civil War is over, but not the feud between Addy and Harriet, until tragedy forces them to come together at last.

❋

Changes for Addy · A Winter Story

The long struggle to reunite Addy's family finally ends, but there is heartache along with the happiness.

HAPPY BIRTHDAY, ADDY!

A SPRINGTIME STORY

BY CONNIE PORTER

ILLUSTRATIONS BRADFORD BROWN

VIGNETTES RENÉE GRAEF, GERI STRIGENZ BOURGET

SCHOLASTIC INC.

NEW YORK   TORONTO   LONDON   AUCKLAND   SYDNEY

PICTURE CREDITS

The following individuals and organizations have generously given permission to reprint
illustrations contained in "Looking Back": pp. 56-57—The William Gladstone Collection,
Westport, Connecticut (mother and child photo); The Historic New Orleans Collection,
Accession no. 1975.93.2 (slaves returning from field); pp. 58-59—Courtesy of Chester County
Historical Society, West Chester, PA (rag doll); Collection of The New-York Historical Society
(children playing); North Wind Picture Archives (wedding ceremony); Sophia Smith
Collection, Smith College (free black girl); pp. 60-61—Massachusetts Commandery, Military
Order of the Loyal Legion and the U.S. Army Military History Institute (drummer boy);
The Museum of the Confederacy, Richmond, Virginia, Photography by Katherine Wetzel
(sewing kit); Photographs and Prints Division, Schomburg Center for Research in Black
Culture, The New York Public Library, Astor, Lenox and Tilden Foundations
(Union soldiers); Courtesy Library of Congress (soldiers returning home).

Edited by Roberta Johnson
Designed by Myland McRevey and Jane S. Varda
Art Directed by Kathleen A. Brown

ISBN 0-590-67729-2

14 13 12 11 10 9 8   8 9/9 0 1/0

Printed in the U.S.A.   23

First Scholastic printing, September 1995

TO MY PARENTS

TABLE OF CONTENTS

POPPA
*Addy's father, whose
dream gives the family
strength.*

MOMMA
*Addy's mother, whose
love helps the family
survive.*

ADDY
*A courageous girl,
smart and strong,
growing up during
the Civil War.*

SAM
*Addy's sixteen-year-old
brother, determined to
be free.*

ESTHER
*Addy's two-year-old
sister.*

SARAH MOORE
Addy's good friend.

M'DEAR
*An elderly woman
who befriends Addy.*

REVEREND DRAKE
*The inspiring
minister at Trinity
A.M.E. Church.*

MR. AND MRS. GOLDEN
*The owners of the boarding
house where the Walkers live.*

DOUBLE DUTCH

The jump ropes slapped on the sidewalk as Addy took her place at the end of the line of girls who were playing Double Dutch after school. Addy had just missed for the fourth time.

"Don't worry," said her good friend Sarah. "Just keep trying. You'll get it. Double Dutch is hard."

Addy agreed. "It sure is. I can jump with one rope just fine. But the minute I try to jump into two, I get all tangled up. The ropes go so fast, I can hardly see them."

"That'll change," said Sarah. "Just don't get discouraged."

In spite of her troubles with Double Dutch, Addy felt happy on this pretty spring day. Poppa had been back with her and Momma for three months. They had moved out of Mrs. Ford's garret and into a boarding house. It was almost like having a big family again, except that Addy's brother Sam and baby sister Esther weren't there. *Maybe that'll change someday, too,* she thought.

"Look it there," Sarah said, pointing up the street. "Ain't that your poppa driving the ice wagon?"

Addy looked where Sarah was pointing.

"That's Poppa!" Addy exclaimed. "Let's go meet him." The girls took off and raced down the block.

"Well, well," Poppa said in his deep voice when the girls reached the wagon. "Look what the wind done blown my way. I reckon you girls could use a nice chunk of ice to cool you down."

"I sure could," said Sarah, panting from the run.

"Me, too," said Addy with a smile.

Poppa got down from his seat. The girls followed him to the back where he opened the doors of the wagon. Inside were huge blocks of ice.

2

Addy could feel a moist coolness come from inside. Poppa slipped on a pair of thick gloves and took an ice pick from his belt. As he chipped away at a block of ice, glittering slivers flew into the air. He handed Sarah and Addy each a piece of ice the size of a small slice of pie.

"If you girls want a ride home, I'm gonna be heading that way in a bit. I got a few stops to make first," Poppa said.

"We'd like to ride. Come on, Sarah," Addy said.

"I can't," said Sarah. "I got to get right straight home and help my momma."

"All right," Addy said. "I'll see you tomorrow." She was disappointed. Sarah often had to help her mother do the washing that she took in to earn money.

Addy and Poppa climbed onto the wagon as Sarah left. Poppa slapped the reins on the horse's back and the wagon moved away from the curb.

Addy sat close to Poppa, sucking on her piece of ice. It was like holding a piece of winter. Addy had to shift it from hand to hand as it slowly melted and dripped. Poppa gave her his huge gloves.

"Wear these," he said, "so your hands won't get cold."

"I wish Sarah ain't have to help her momma so much," Addy said as she put the gloves on.

"I wish she didn't neither," Poppa said, "but her family need the money." He shook his head. "I never did expect things to be easy in freedom, but I didn't think things would be so hard either."

Addy looked at Poppa. His big smile had melted away. His face looked serious.

"When me and Momma first got here, I didn't like Philadelphia at all," Addy said softly. "Momma worked real hard, and I spent most of my time alone in our room. I was missing you and Sam and Esther something awful. But Momma kept saying things was gonna get better. It was gonna take time for things to change."

"Sometimes it seem like change is as slow as this here tired old horse," Poppa sighed. "But at least in Philadelphia, things can change for the better."

"That's true," Addy said, finishing her ice and removing Poppa's gloves. "When we was down on

4

the plantation, there was no chance for things to change."

"Slavery was draining the life out of all of us," said Poppa. "That's one reason I knew we had to take our freedom."

Addy spread out her arms. "Here in Philadelphia, it seem like my world getting bigger and bigger. Sometimes I can't believe I really go to school, that I can read and write and do my figures. I used to dream about it, but now it's real. And look at us, Poppa. We riding around the city on this big wagon! This is much better than worming tobacco plants."

Addy saw a smile ease back onto Poppa's face.

Poppa said, "There *is* some things better here. You going to school, me and your momma getting *paid* for our work, and we got a nice room at the boarding house."

"Even though Sam and Esther ain't with us yet," Addy said, "you being here done made things much better for me and Momma."

"But I want them to be even better," Poppa responded. "Hauling ice don't take nothing but muscle. I'm a good carpenter. I got a good mind.

*"Here in Philadelphia, it seem like my world
getting bigger and bigger," said Addy.*

I can build anything. Every carpenter job I try to get, they say they don't hire colored folks. Ain't that something, Addy? When we was in slavery, I was a carpenter. Now that I'm free, I find out these white people up North think a colored man ain't good enough or smart enough to drive a nail."

"That ain't fair," Addy said.

"Sure ain't," Poppa said. "But that's the way it is."

Poppa made two deliveries before he came to his last stop at Natkin's Confectionery Shop. Addy could see a group of white girls about her age sitting at a table eating ice cream. She had walked by this shop once with Sarah, and Sarah had told her they sold ice cream there. Back then, Addy had not even known what ice cream was, but at a church social a few weeks later, Addy had her first taste of it. She loved it! It was creamy and sweet and cold. Without thinking, Addy blurted out to Poppa, "It sure would be good to have some ice cream now."

As soon as the words had flown out of her mouth, Addy felt awful. She shouldn't ask Poppa to spend money on fancy treats, and she also knew that this shop didn't serve black people. She looked again at the group of girls talking happily inside. Poppa glanced where Addy was looking. He didn't say anything as he climbed down from the wagon.

Addy watched Poppa lift a huge block of ice with a pair of large tongs. He rested it on his shoulder, headed down the alley, and went in the side door of the confectionery. On his way out, Poppa stopped to talk to a white man who gave Poppa a friendly pat on the shoulder.

"Was that Mr. Natkin?" asked Addy.

Poppa climbed back onto the wagon. "Yes," said Poppa. "I'm telling you, Addy, this is some kinda freedom. I can deliver ice to make ice cream, but I can't even buy my own daughter a dish of it."

"That's all right," Addy said. "I don't like it, anyway."

Poppa looked at her out of the corner of his eye. Addy could tell he didn't believe her. "Let me make sure that door is closed," he said, jumping from the wagon.

When Poppa returned, he was carrying something. "Look here at what was in the trash," he said. "It's a busted-up ice cream freezer. I bet

I can fix it up. Then we'll make our own ice cream." Poppa gave Addy a playful nudge. "Won't that be nice?" he asked.

"It would be," Addy said.

Poppa tugged on the reins, and the wagon gave a slow lurch forward.

Addy and Poppa rode on in silence. She was thinking, *Momma, Poppa, and I and all the colored people got a strange kind of freedom here in Philadelphia. There are jobs we can't get and shops we can't eat at just because of the color of our skin. It ain't fair.* When Addy thought of it, she felt just as dizzy as she had standing before the spinning loops of the Double Dutch ropes. Being a black girl in Philadelphia was like being outside the loops of those ropes. Inside was a world Addy wanted to enter. But right now, she was standing on the outside looking in. How would she be able to jump into that other world?

SUNSHINE

 When Addy came home from school
the next day, a small wagon loaded
with furniture was in front of the tall
boarding house. Boarders often moved in and out.
Mr. and Mrs. Golden, who owned the boarding
house, rented out five rooms, but Addy was the only
child in the house. She looked carefully at the things
in the wagon, hoping to see something belonging to
a child, maybe a doll sticking out of a crate. But all
she saw was furniture.

Mr. Golden came out of the front door. Addy
thought that his name was perfect for him. His skin
was golden brown. "Good afternoon to you, Addy.
How are you today?"

"Good afternoon, Mr. Golden," Addy said. "I'm doing fine. Who's moving in?"

Mr. Golden sat down on the front step and wiped his neck with a handkerchief. "By the looks of all this furniture, you'd think a family of ten was moving in, but it's just one person—my mother."

"Oh," Addy said, a little disappointed that she wouldn't be getting a playmate. "Would you like some help?"

"No, but thank you kindly," Mr. Golden said, getting up from the step. He went over to the wagon.

Addy went up to her family's room on the second floor. She flopped onto her bed and reached for her doll, Ida Bean, who had been lying on her pillow. Addy loved Ida Bean. She could cuddle with Ida and tell her secrets. But even with Ida to keep her company, Addy still felt lonely during the long afternoons. All the adults in the boarding house were at work. Mrs. Golden was busy making supper for everyone and didn't want to be disturbed. Momma and Poppa didn't get home until late. Sometimes they didn't get home in time for the dinner Mrs. Golden served. On those days, Addy

11

still joined the other boarders for supper in the dining room.

This evening was one of those times, so when Mrs. Golden rang her bell, Addy went down to the dining room by herself. She took her place at one of the two tables. Four other boarders sat at that table, but they didn't pay attention to Addy. They were talking about the trouble black people were facing on the streetcars.

"Did you see today's paper?" Mrs. Golden asked. "There was almost a riot on a streetcar downtown. Three colored people were hurt."

12

"I'm getting too scared to even ride the streetcars at all," one woman said.

A man at the table joined in, "Well, I heard a conductor threw a colored man off the Pine Street streetcar and broke his leg."

"If they'd just let us sit inside, there wouldn't be all this trouble," another young woman at the table added.

"That'll be the day," said Mr. Golden sourly. "I'll be an old man before I see that change come."

Their talk scared Addy. The longer she listened, the less she was interested in her supper. She began playing with the napkin ring, and she only picked at her dinner of oxtail stew and mashed carrots.

napkin in a napkin ring

After dinner, Addy headed back to her room. She was halfway up the stairs when she heard a bird singing. Quietly, Addy tiptoed back down the stairs. The bird's beautiful song was like a trail that Addy followed down the narrow hall. The trail stopped at the open door of a room at the end. The room was unlit. The faint light from the hall was the only brightness in it.

At first, Addy saw only her own shadow in the

room. But as her eyes got used to the dimness, she saw a cage hanging before the window. In it was a small, yellow bird, sitting on a perch singing out happily. She stood at the door for a minute, enjoying its song.

Suddenly a woman's voice interrupted, "You can come in, child."

Addy was so startled, she jumped. She hadn't seen anyone in the darkened room. She moved a few steps inside. The woman lit a kerosene lamp, and Addy saw the furniture she had seen on the wagon earlier in the day. The woman sat in a high-backed rocker next to the cage.

"Good evening, ma'am," Addy said.

kerosene lamp   "I'm Addy Walker. Me and my momma and poppa live upstairs. You Mr. Golden's momma?"

"That's right," the woman answered. "Come on in and meet my bird, Sunny."

Addy went over closer to the cage. It was then that she saw the woman's eyes. The colored parts of her eyes, the irises, were covered with a cloudy whiteness. Addy stood staring at the woman.

14

"Didn't know I was blind, did you?"
Mrs. Golden asked.

Addy answered quickly, "No, ma'am. If you
blind, how did you know I was standing outside
your door?"

"I got plenty of ways of seeing," answered
Mrs. Golden. "I heard your footsteps. They were
soft as a whisper, and they were spaced close
together, so I could tell you were a child. How old
are you, Addy?" Mrs. Golden asked. "When is
your birthday?"

"I'm nine," Addy said. "But I ain't really sure
about when my birthday is. I was born in the spring.
My momma know that much." Addy felt ashamed
that she didn't know her birthday. Her seatmate at
school, Harriet, knew when her birthday was. On
that day, Harriet's mother had sent fancy raisin tarts
for the whole class.

"That's a shame you don't know your birthday,"
Mrs. Golden said. "Just listening to you talk, I think
you were born into slavery."

"Yes, ma'am," Addy said. "How did you know?"

"Well, most slaves don't know their birthday,"
Mrs. Golden continued. "I was born right here in

Philadelphia, but my parents were born into slavery over one hundred years ago. I'm an old woman, you know. I was there the day God invented dirt."

Addy looked at Mrs. Golden in disbelief.

Mrs. Golden laughed so light and high, it made the room seem brighter. Addy joined in with her laughter.

"You real funny, ma'am," Addy said. "My brother Sam would like you. He like riddles and jokes."

"Your brother?" Mrs. Golden said. "You didn't mention him. Does he live here, too?"

"No, ma'am," Addy explained sadly. "We don't know where Sam is. He might still be a slave, but he wanted to be a soldier. He and my poppa were sold off the plantation. Then my momma and me ran away up here. We had to leave my baby sister Esther on the plantation when we left. But someday, we gonna all be together again."

"Slavery has taken a lot away from colored people," Mrs. Golden said. "If we want to get some of it back, we're going to have to take it. It's going to be some time before your family gets back together. But I know one thing you can take for yourself right

16

now, Addy. Whenever you want, you can choose
a special day and claim it for your birthday."

Addy had never thought about this before.
"That's a good idea!" she exclaimed. "I want me
a really special day. I want me a perfect day for
my birthday."

"Now I've told you I've been around a long
time, and I never saw such a thing as a perfect day,"
Mrs. Golden said.

"How about the day that God invented dirt?"
Addy joked.

"Oh, no, no," Mrs. Golden said. "Even that
wasn't perfect. But there *is* something special in
every day."

"How will I know what day is right for my
birthday?" asked Addy.

"You'll just know," answered Mrs. Golden.
"When that almost-perfect day comes along, it'll be
meant just for you. Now, the day God invented birds
was extra special, close to perfect, and I was there
for that, too."

Sunny seemed to understand what Mrs. Golden
was saying. He sang happily with his head cocked
back and his breast puffed out.

*"Whenever you want, you can choose a special day and
claim it for your birthday," said Mrs. Golden.*

18

"Mrs. Golden, why your bird in that cage? It seem like he would be sad and lonesome in there all by himself," Addy said.

Mrs. Golden closed her eyes for a moment before she answered. "I can tell you're a smart girl. You think about things. I do think Sunny is lonely sometimes. I think I can hear it in his song. But we keep each other company. When I hear him singing out from his soul, it brings sunshine into my life."

Addy thought about that. "But he still locked up."

"Oh, child," answered Mrs. Golden. "That cage can't contain Sunny's spirit. It soars right out from behind those bars. That's what's important for all of us. To let our souls sing out."

"Sometimes it's hard to do that, you know," Addy replied, "to let yourself sing out if you feeling lonely or sad."

"Sure is," Mrs. Golden said, looking right at her. "I'll tell you, Addy. When you first spoke to me tonight, I could hear a touch of loneliness in your voice. But even then, I could hear you singing out."

Addy looked away from Mrs. Golden. Addy knew she was blind, but she felt like Mrs. Golden was looking deep inside her.

"Well, I better be going," Addy said. "I still have lessons to do, Mrs. Golden."

"Don't be a stranger at my door, now," Mrs. Golden said. "Come visit me and Sunny whenever you'd like. And one more thing. Please call me M'dear. That's what my family calls me."

"I will," replied Addy. "I will."

CHAPTER
THREE

BITTER MEDICINE

During the next week, Addy stopped
by M'dear's room each day when she
came home from school.

"Good afternoon," M'dear would call to her
before she even reached M'dear's door. Addy usually
did her lessons in M'dear's room, and sometimes
M'dear had a treat of benne candy for her when she
finished. Addy savored the crispy, sugary wafers
filled with sesame seeds while she listened to stories
M'dear told her. M'dear told Addy that her father
had been a soldier in the Revolutionary War, and
that when she had been a chore girl working on
Society Hill, Thomas Jefferson had visited a house
where she worked. Addy loved the stories M'dear

21

told and was happy that M'dear was her friend.

Addy still spent Saturdays by herself because Poppa and Momma had to work. But this Saturday was going to be different. Momma had told Addy on Thursday, "I know you enjoy M'dear's company, but she's an old woman. She need her rest. Why don't you ask Sarah to come over on Saturday morning?"

"Do you really mean it, Momma?" Addy had asked. Momma had never let Sarah come over to play before.

"Me and Poppa think you should play together more than you do," Momma said.

Poppa was sitting on the floor piecing together the ice cream freezer he had found. "Maybe Sarah can help you pick a day for your birthday," he said. "Remember, when you pick it, Addy, I'm gonna make you ice cream. And you better hurry. I just about got this old freezer fixed."

When Saturday morning came, Addy couldn't wait for Sarah to arrive. The night before, Momma had saved sweet cornbread for Addy and Sarah to share. Momma said they could have that and some milk for a treat. Addy spread an old blanket on the floor. She placed two small plates, spoons, cups, and the cornbread on it. Then Addy eagerly watched out the window for Sarah. When she saw Sarah coming up the street, Addy thundered down the stairs to meet her.

Sarah was carrying a bag, and she had a smile on her face.

"What you got in the sack?" Addy asked Sarah.

"It's a surprise," Sarah said, as Addy led her inside and up the stairs. When they got to the room, Sarah looked at the spread on the floor. "This real nice, Addy," Sarah said. "It's like having a picnic inside."

"I thought you'd like it," Addy said as she poured the milk into their cups. "You're never gonna guess what Momma and Poppa said. You can help me pick a special day for my birthday."

"I think you should pick it all by yourself," said Sarah.

"I guess you right," Addy responded, taking a sip of milk. "I just can't think of a day I want. Don't none seem right enough."

After they had finished, Sarah held up her sack in front of Addy and said, "Keep your eyes closed and reach inside the sack for a surprise."

"Oh, Sarah!" Addy cried as she pulled out a coil of rope.

"I thought we could practice some Double Dutch," said Sarah. "My momma have so many clotheslines from her washing that my poppa cut me this extra piece for us to jump with."

The girls rushed outside, where Sarah wound the middle of the rope around a lamppost. She held the two ends in her hands and began twirling.

Addy felt a little dizzy as she watched the two loops of the rope cross over one another. Again and again she tried to jump in, but Addy's feet always got tangled in the ropes as soon as she did. Sarah continued to encourage her. "That was a good try, Addy."

Addy was feeling discouraged when she heard M'dear say, "Addy, take your time. Watch the ropes, but listen, too."

Addy looked up to see M'dear sitting at the window. Addy introduced Sarah to M'dear, who asked Sarah to start the ropes again.

"Now listen to those ropes," M'dear coached Addy. "They're singing out a rhythm. Hear it,

Addy? 'Tip-tap-tip-tap, tip-tap-tip-tap.' Jump to that rhythm. You can do it."

Addy had never listened to the ropes before. She had only watched them. Now she rocked back and forth before the twirling ropes, listening, getting her body set to their rhythm. Then she jumped in. She jumped four times before she missed. She had never done so well!

"You getting it," Sarah said. "That was much better."

Addy was encouraged. "Did you see me, M'dear?"

"I saw," M'dear said. "I saw."

Sarah started twirling the ropes again. Addy's hands were sweating with anticipation. *I can do it. I can do it,* she repeated to herself. Addy watched the ropes and listened. Tip-tap-tip-tap. Tip-tap-tip-tap. When she was ready, she leapt in between the loops. She was jumping! Eight times in a row. Ten. Twelve. She was losing count. A big smile burst onto Addy's face. Sarah shrieked with delight. Then the ropes twisted around Addy's feet.

Sarah rushed to Addy and gave her a hug. "I knew you could do it, Addy. You was great!"

"I can't believe it," Addy said happily. "I finally got it." She turned to the window, but M'dear was gone.

Addy jumped rope for a while longer. Then Sarah had her turn. When they got tired, they went inside to M'dear's room.

M'dear's door was open, but she was not sitting in her usual place by the window. Instead, she was lying down with a wet cloth on her forehead. Sunny was silent.

"M'dear, you feel all right?" Addy asked softly.

"I was just resting," answered M'dear. "I have a terrible headache, and I've run out of medicine."

"I'll go to the druggist and get you some more," Addy offered. "It's only a few blocks from here. Sarah will go with me."

"If you're sure it wouldn't be any trouble," M'dear said.

"We'd be glad to go," Addy assured her, taking the blue bottle from the table next to M'dear's bed. "We'll be back real quick."

M'dear gave Addy fifty cents. "Get yourselves a treat while you're out getting my medicine," M'dear said. "And bring back the change."

Addy and Sarah went straight to the drug store, but the clerk said he was out of the medicine M'dear needed. The girls left the shop.

"Now what do we do?" asked Sarah in a worried voice.

"I know where there's another drug store on Pebble Avenue," Addy said. "I saw it when I was on the ice wagon with Poppa the other day."

"But Pebble Avenue is miles from here," said Sarah.

"We can take a streetcar," said Addy. "We'll be there in no time."

"I don't think that's such a good idea," Sarah said. "You know we can't ride most streetcars."

"But we *got* to get M'dear's medicine," Addy insisted. "I know which streetcars colored people can ride."

Sarah thought for a minute. "But they dangerous," she protested.

"Not if we stick together," said Addy. "Come on."

Addy and Sarah walked one block to the avenue. They waited only a few minutes before a streetcar came, pulled by two horses. Like the other black riders, Addy and Sarah had to ride on the outside platform. Only whites could ride inside and sit in the seats.

As the horses took off, Addy and Sarah held tightly to the railing. From the first day Addy had arrived in Philadelphia, she had wanted to ride a streetcar. Now here she was! The horses built up speed, and Addy felt a warm breeze sweeping past her. The city whizzed by—the row houses, the markets, the churches. They were a blur kissed by the green of budding trees. As the streetcar slowed, the city came back into focus. When the streetcar stopped for more passengers, the white people paid their fares first. They moved inside, where there were plenty of seats. The black people who came aboard had to squeeze their way onto the outside platform, which was getting crowded. Addy looked at Sarah, who looked worried.

"We almost there," Addy assured her.

The car pulled away so suddenly, the man next to Addy lost his balance and stepped on her foot. The people on the platform were crowded so tightly together now that Addy couldn't feel the breeze as the streetcar gained speed. Addy was relieved when they arrived at their stop and could get off.

The drug store was just a block away from the streetcar stop. The girls took off in a hurry, anxious to get the medicine and return to M'dear. When they reached the store, they found a long line of people waiting at the counter. Addy and Sarah went to the end of the line.

"We'll be on our way in a few minutes," Addy said to Sarah.

The girls inched their way forward in the line. Ten minutes passed before they were up to the counter. Before Addy could open her mouth to ask

29

for the medicine, a man approached the counter. The clerk ignored Addy and waited on him.

"We was next," Sarah whispered to Addy.

"I know," Addy said softly. "Maybe he used to waiting on grown folks first. He probably ain't see us. He gonna wait on us next."

When the clerk finished with the man, Addy started to say, "We'd like to get . . . " Before she could finish her sentence, the clerk walked away to wait on a white girl who had just walked in the door.

"You can't say he didn't see us this time," Sarah said.

Addy knew that Sarah was right. They watched in surprise as the clerk waited on the girl, who was no older than they were. He talked nicely to her as he filled her order. After the girl handed him her money, the clerk gave her back the change, counting it out in her hand.

Finally the clerk came over to Addy. "What do *you* want?" he asked in a stern voice that startled her.

Addy handed him the medicine bottle and asked for another just like it.

"Do you have money?" he asked.

Addy thought that was a strange question. *Why*

would I be here if I ain't have money? she thought. She tried to hand the clerk her money.

"Put it on the counter," he demanded.

Addy glanced at Sarah, who was looking at the floor. As Addy placed the money on the counter, she felt her face getting hot. She was angry and hurt. This was how her master had talked to her on the plantation.

After Addy put the money on the counter, the clerk took it and got the medicine. Then, instead of handing Addy her change, he slapped it down on the counter. Some of it rolled onto the floor. Sarah scrambled to get it. Without saying a word, Addy picked up the medicine and the girls left the shop.

Addy and Sarah started down the avenue, walking hand in hand, to wait for a streetcar to take them back across town.

"That man treated us so bad," Addy said.

"Because we colored," Sarah added. "Some white folks think they're better than us."

"But that's not right," protested Addy, hurt and confused.

"No, it ain't," agreed Sarah. "But things ain't always right."

When they got back to the streetcar stop, a large crowd was waiting impatiently. The first streetcar that came along was packed. It didn't even stop, and some of the people waiting on the corner began to grumble.

"We *gotta* get on this next one," Addy said anxiously. "M'dear waiting for her medicine."

It was twenty minutes before another car came. It stopped and Addy, Sarah, and the rest of the black passengers got on, crowding the platform. As the streetcar pulled out, they were packed so closely that Addy didn't have to hold onto the railing. She held tightly to the bottle of medicine.

At the next stop, the conductor yelled out, "White passengers only!"

A white man made his way through the crowd and got on. He pushed through the black passengers on the platform and sat down in one of the empty seats inside.

"That's not fair," a black man in overalls called

up from the street. "We've been waiting for a car for an hour."

A woman standing near the man added, "There's plenty of room if you let us ride inside."

"I don't make the rules," the conductor replied. "You'll have to wait for the next car."

"We won't wait!" the black man in the overalls yelled. He and some of the other people who had been waiting pushed their way onto the car.

The conductor's voice boomed, "Get off of this car! Get off!"

Addy felt her heart beating fast. She looked for Sarah, but Sarah had been pushed past her. As Addy turned, she saw the conductor pushing through the passengers toward the people who had just gotten on the streetcar. Some of them jumped off, but the man in the overalls didn't. He held onto the railing. When the conductor reached him, he grabbed the man by the straps of his overalls and pulled at him until the man lost his grip and fell to the street.

Then the conductor turned to the black people on the platform. "Now, all of you colored people, out!" he bellowed. His face was red with fury. "Every last one of you!"

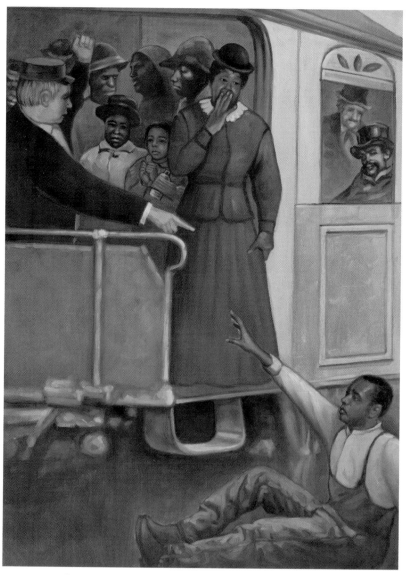

*"Now, all of you colored people, out!" the conductor
bellowed. "Every last one of you!"*

34

"We already paid our fare," one woman protested.

"I don't care," he screamed. "I'll call the police if every last one of you doesn't get off right now!"

Addy felt pushing from all sides. A sharp elbow hit her shoulder. Someone trampled over her feet. Addy was caught up in the crowd, and before she knew it, she was swept right off the platform. She fell to the ground, ripping a hole in her stocking and scraping her knee. She watched the streetcar pull away from the stop with no one on the platform and plenty of empty seats inside.

Sarah rushed up to her. "Addy, is you all right?"

"I guess so," Addy said. "At least I didn't drop M'dear's medicine."

"I don't want to get back on no streetcar," said Sarah.

"Don't worry about that," said Addy. "There ain't no more money for the fare anyway. We used up everything M'dear gave us on the two rides we already took."

"How far is it to home?" Sarah asked.

"It's a long way from here," Addy said. "A long way."

BROTHERLY LOVE

It was late afternoon when Addy and Sarah finally made it back to the boarding house. As they trudged down the hall, M'dear called out, "Addy, is that you and your friend?"

"It's us," Addy answered. She tried not to sound as discouraged as she felt.

"Come right on in here," M'dear said with relief in her voice. "I was so worried about you, I was thinking of coming after you myself."

Addy and Sarah went into M'dear's room. Addy tried to dust off her dress and hide the hole in her stocking, but then she remembered that M'dear couldn't see them.

"Addy, what took you so long?" M'dear asked.

Addy and Sarah glanced at one another.

"The druggist in the neighborhood didn't have the medicine, so we had to go to another store," Addy explained. Her voice was trembling a little. She was telling the truth, at least part of it. When Addy handed M'dear the medicine, M'dear reached for Addy's hand and held it in her own. M'dear's eyes looked right into Addy's.

"There's something else," M'dear said gently. "I can tell by your voice."

Reluctantly, Addy started telling the story. When she got to the part about being forced off the streetcar, Addy said, "We was just minding our own business, and the conductor threw all of us colored people off. That ain't right."

"No, it's not right," M'dear said.

"I don't understand," Sarah piped in. "I thought colored people in the North supposed to be free. But we're in the North and we ain't free."

M'dear was quiet for a moment, and then she answered, "You're right, Sarah, we still have to fight for our freedom here in the North. That's because some people are prejudiced. Prejudice blinds people.

It doesn't allow them to see people for who they really are. That conductor who mistreated you girls is blind, blinder than me."

"I don't see why Philadelphia is called the 'City of Brotherly Love,'" Addy said. "The druggist across town didn't want to wait on us because we colored. We can't ride inside the streetcars because we colored. We can't go into Natkin's Confectionery to get ice cream because we colored. My poppa can't even get a job as a carpenter because he colored. There ain't any brotherly love in this city, and it ain't ever gonna change."

"Why do you feel things won't ever change?" M'dear asked.

"Because we can't change the color of our skin," Addy answered.

"Well, you're right about that," M'dear agreed. "We *can't* change the color of our skin. But don't let prejudice make you its prisoner. Remember Sunny. His spirit goes beyond his cage with every note he sings." Gently, M'dear put her hand on Addy's cheek. "You have to keep right on living, right on singing your song."

38

☀

After Sarah had gone home, Poppa stopped by the boarding house to take Addy with him on his last deliveries. As they rolled along on the slow-moving wagon, Poppa asked Addy how the day had gone with Sarah. Addy told him about their picnic and Double Dutch, but not about the trip to the druggist's and the trouble on the streetcar. Poppa had a solemn look on his face, and Addy didn't think he needed to hear any bad news.

"I looked for a job today on my meal break," Poppa said. "I heard they was hiring carpenters for a warehouse going up over near the docks. When I went there, it was the same old story. The foreman told me he didn't hire colored folks."

Addy encouraged Poppa, "Well, that man was blind. He couldn't see you for who you is, one of the best carpenters in all of Philadelphia."

Poppa put an arm around Addy's shoulders and smiled. He said, "Well, listen to you. Don't you sound like a wise old lady?"

"It's true, though, Poppa," Addy said. "Somebody gonna hire you for carpenter work, someday. I just know they will."

"I hope you right, Addy," said Poppa.

On Poppa's last stop, Addy waited in the wagon while Poppa hauled the heavy blocks of ice inside. She heard a bird start singing. It reminded her of Sunny, and Addy turned to see where the bird was. She didn't see it, but when she turned, she saw a sign posted on a building next to the one Poppa had gone in. The sign read, *"CARPENTERS WANTED, APPLY WITHIN."* Addy jumped down from the wagon to find Poppa. He was coming out of the building just then. Addy rushed to him and told him about the sign.

"You should go in and see what they have to say," Addy said.

Poppa stood for a moment looking at Addy. "I know what they gonna say, but I'll ask anyway."

Poppa walked up to the steps of the building and knocked firmly on the door. Addy watched him from the sidewalk.

A white man with a beard answered the door. His beard was filled with sawdust.

"My name is Ben Walker, and I come to see about the carpenter job," Poppa said in a strong, sure voice.

"My name is Ben Walker, and I come to see about the carpenter job,"
Poppa said in a strong, sure voice.

41

"I'm Miles Roberts. Have you done carpentry before?" the man asked.

"I sure have, Mr. Roberts," Poppa said. "I'll tell you right now that I can't read or write yet, but I know how to work wood. I can do everything from build a stairway or a fence to lay a floor or frame a window. I got plenty of knowledge right up here." Poppa tapped his finger to his head. "And I got a strong pair of hands. All I'm asking for is a chance."

"Do you have your own tools?" Mr. Roberts asked.

Poppa answered, "I got a few—a hammer, a saw, and a plane."

Mr. Roberts rubbed his beard. "I'll tell you what," he said. "Come back here on Monday morning at six o'clock sharp, and I'll put you to work."

"Yes, sir," Poppa said heartily. "I'll be here."

Mr. Roberts shook Poppa's hand and shut the door. Poppa leaped down the steps, swept Addy up in his arms, and spun her around.

When he put her down, Addy said, "I told you, Poppa. Someday somebody was gonna see you for who you really is!"

She and Poppa climbed back in the wagon.
Poppa grinned. "Your momma is gonna be so
happy," he said.

As they headed down the street atop the wagon,
the sun was setting. Poppa began to whistle a song
Addy had never heard before. It was a song full
of hope.

CHANGES IN THE WIND

Addy was happy when she woke up on Sunday morning. Momma and Poppa wouldn't have to work. It was a sunny spring day, and Poppa would start his carpenter job tomorrow.

After breakfast, Addy and Momma and Poppa went to church. Reverend Drake preached about being ready because a change was coming. He said the war would be over any day now, and when it was, a change would come sweeping through the country like the gusty winds of spring. Addy hoped that what the Reverend said might be true.

After church, Addy and her parents went back to the boarding house to eat dinner with the other boarders. Then they went to Washington Square. Addy brought the jump rope Sarah had given her, and Momma and Poppa turned it while she showed them how well she could jump Double Dutch.

"How in the world did you learn to jump rope so good?" Poppa asked with pride.

Addy kept jumping as she answered, "Sarah and M'dear taught me."

"I can understand Sarah teaching you, but how could M'dear?" Momma asked. "She blind."

"She's blind, but she has a way of seeing things real clear," Addy said. "She's been teaching me how to see with my ears and sing with my heart."

"Are you riddling me?" asked Poppa. "You sound just like your brother."

"No, it's not a riddle, Poppa," Addy said. "M'dear know all about the world. She been around since God invented dirt!"

As the afternoon turned to evening, Addy and Poppa and Momma headed home.

"When are you gonna pick your birthday, Addy?" Momma asked as they walked along. "Your poppa's got that ice cream freezer fixed and ready."

"I'm waiting for an almost-perfect day," answered Addy. "But I think it's coming soon."

"Well, it better hurry," said Momma. "I'm getting real hungry for ice cream."

※

That night Addy was awakened suddenly by a noise out in the street. She didn't know what it was at first. Poppa had already jumped up from the bed. He was looking out the window.

"What's all that fuss out there?" Momma asked sleepily.

Addy was fully awake by then. She heard three big booms that rattled the panes of the window.

"That's cannon fire," Poppa said. "It's got to be coming from the harbor."

Suddenly, there were more booms, and then popping noises that sounded like shots cracking through the air.

"Maybe the war's come to Philadelphia," said Momma with alarm.

Poppa started to answer, but the sound of people cheering, whistles blowing, and church bells ringing drowned out his words. Addy's heart started beating faster. *All this noise, and at this time of night. I bet I know what's happened!* Addy thought. She jumped out of bed and joined Poppa at the window. Down below, the street was beginning to fill with people.

"Momma, get up!" Addy urged as she turned from the window to look at Momma. "I think the war is over!" Addy started jumping up and down.

"I think Addy right, Ruth. That's got to be it," Poppa said. He went over to Momma. She was crying, and so was Poppa. Addy went to the bed and put her arms around them.

"Don't cry," Addy said. But Addy was so happy, she thought she was going to cry, too.

Poppa and Momma dried their eyes, and Momma said, "This mean we gonna get a chance to see Esther and Sam again. This the day we all been waiting for."

"Come on, let's get dressed and go on out," Poppa said. "I know I can't go back to sleep now."

They all dressed quickly. As they rushed downstairs, they met some of the other boarders, half-dressed and talking excitedly. Addy, Poppa, and Momma went outside.

"Momma, get up!" Addy urged. "I think the war is over!"

Someone in the crowded street yelled, "General Lee has surrendered!"

Another cried, "The war is over! The North has won!"

Addy looked back to the house and saw M'dear at a window.

"M'dear!" Addy called over the noise of the crowd. "I wish you could see all this!"

"In my way, I can," M'dear called back.

Poppa took Addy's hand and led her and Momma into the street. As they joined the crowd of people, someone handed them lanterns and banners. Hundreds of people, young and old, black and white, filled the street and sidewalks. They were crying and hugging, laughing and cheering. Some were still in their nightclothes. They were beating pie tins and pots and pans. One man beat a drum and another played a fiddle. Firecrackers popped all around them. Addy looked up to see flags and red, white, and blue bunting draped on buildings.

This just like a dream, Addy thought. She looked up at the huge banners being held up on sticks high above the crowd. The banners waved gently in the

breeze, and Addy began reading them aloud. *"LINCOLN AND LIBERTY!"* *"ONE PEOPLE, ONE COUNTRY."* *"AMERICA: NORTH AND SOUTH, UNITED AGAIN!"* This was the day she had been waiting for. It was not perfect. If it were, her brother and sister would be right there with her, but this was the best day she could imagine without them.

She turned to Momma and Poppa. "I want today to be my birthday," Addy said.

"You picked one fine day for it," Poppa replied. "We should go on back home and have a party. The freezer I fixed is just waiting to make ice cream."

As they made their way back home, Addy spotted some familiar faces in the crowd—Sarah and her parents. Addy rushed up to Sarah and threw her arms around her.

"I can't believe it," Sarah cried out. "The war really over."

"At last!" Addy said. "And guess what?" She didn't give Sarah a chance to answer. "I'm having my birthday right now, and a party, and you and your momma and poppa got to come!"

"Addy!" laughed Sarah. "You sure picked a good birthday. The ninth of April is a day nobody will ever forget!"

When Addy's and Sarah's families arrived at the boarding house, every room was lit up. They went inside to find Mr. and Mrs. Golden, M'dear, and the boarders talking in the dining room. Poppa made his way through the room shaking hands and hugging everyone. Then he hopped up on a chair and made an announcement, "Today is my daughter's tenth birthday, and you all invited to a party right here in this dining room. I'm gonna make a freezer full of ice cream!"

Everyone cheered and Momma said, "Addy, you and Sarah stay out of the way till we get things set up for the party."

"Momma, can we go out and jump rope till then?" asked Addy.

"Yes, but stay on the sidewalk right in front of the house," Momma said. "And Poppa, get started on that ice cream. If you don't, we'll be having it for breakfast."

Outside, Addy and Sarah took turns jumping rope. Addy jumped better than she ever had before.

Some people who were coming back from the celebration joined in their game, jumping in and missing and then trying again. Two strangers offered to turn the ropes for the girls so that Addy and Sarah could jump together. Other people stood by, clapping to the rhythm of their jumping.

"Listen to the ropes," Addy told them. "They singing out a rhythm."

It didn't seem long before Momma came out to tell Addy and Sarah that the ice cream was ready and the party would be starting. The girls went inside.

When Addy entered the dining room, she gasped. "Oh, Momma. It's so beautiful."

Mrs. Golden and Momma had set the tables with pretty bowls and lavender glasses. There were shiny copper pitchers of ginger pop. In the center of each table were flowers. Poppa carried in the ice cream freezer. He removed the paddle from inside and began dishing out scoops of ice cream. Mrs. Golden brought in two cherry pies from the pie safe.

"I was saving these for tomorrow's dinner," Mrs. Golden said, "but tonight is a real celebration for Addy and for all of us. We'll have them now."

Momma led Addy to one table, and there at her place was a tin of benne candies from M'dear. M'dear handed her something else wrapped in tissue paper. "You sure did pick a special day for your birthday," said M'dear. "This is from Sunny and me."

Addy opened the gift to find two of Sunny's bright yellow feathers tied together with a bow. Addy held them gently, a bit of bright sunshine in the palm of her hand.

"Thank you," Addy said. She kissed M'dear and pinned the feathers in her hair.

"Let these remind you to always let your spirit sing out," said M'dear.

"I will," promised Addy. "I will."

LOOKING BACK 1864

A Peek Into the Past

This photo was treasured by one Union soldier who fought in the Civil War.

When Addy was growing up, babies were born
at home. *Midwives* were usually called in to help.
Midwives are women trained to help other women with
childbirth. In slave families, older women, such as aunts
or grandmothers, were often experienced midwives and
helped younger women deliver their babies. People
didn't know as much about good health and medical
care in Addy's time as we do now, so many mothers
and babies died during childbirth or shortly after.

56

On farms and plantations in the South, enslaved women had to work even when they had young babies, so older girls or elderly women usually took care of the infants. On some plantations, mothers could bring their babies with them to the fields. They often carried their babies on their backs as they worked.

As the babies grew older and became toddlers, they played with the other children, both black and white, who lived on the plantation. Slave children often became friends with the children of the plantation's master. Sometimes these friendships lasted for many years. But black children soon learned that they were treated differently from white children. Sometimes enslaved children were told to call the master's children "young master" and "young mistress."

As the enslaved and white children on plantations got older, their lives became more separate. Many white children went to school, but it was against the law for slave children to go to school in much of the South. Instead, slave children had to start doing chores when they were about eight years old.

Slave children had to carry drinking water to field workers, gather wood, and tend the garden, among other chores. This collage, made in the mid-1800s, shows slaves returning from a cotton field.

A rag doll made in the 1800s.

When enslaved children weren't working, they were allowed to play. Boys loved marbles, and girls loved to play with their dolls and to jump rope. Toys were simple and homemade. Dolls might have been made from corn husks or rags. Hide and seek, running and jumping games, and ball games also were popular. Children still enjoy some of the singing games played by slave and free children in Addy's time. "Ring Around the Rosie" and "Sally Walker" are two of them.

Slave children and their parents also liked to tell stories about Brer Rabbit, a clever rabbit who loved to play tricks. These stories were based on African tales about a hare named Wakaima. Brer Rabbit stories are still told today and are an important part of American folklore.

Enslaved children playing together.

By the time enslaved children became teenagers, they were treated as adults. They worked long hours, just like their parents. Most married in their late teens

After the Civil War ended, thousands of formerly enslaved couples were married.

and started families of their own. Before the end of the Civil War, marriages between slaves were not legal. So enslaved people developed their own marriage customs. For example, "jumping the broom" was part of many slave weddings. A couple might jump over a broom to end the ceremony.

Slave owners often ignored slave marriages and separated couples by selling off the husband or wife. Most couples who were allowed to stay together formed long and lasting marriages. When the Civil War ended, large wedding ceremonies took place in the South in which 50 or 100 couples who were former slaves were married at the same time.

In most areas of the North, both black and white children could go to public school—though they usually went to separate, or *segregated*, schools. In most states, children

A free black girl of school age.

59

weren't required to go to school by law, as they are now, though most children attended school for at least a few years. City girls and boys usually quit going to school after the age of twelve or thirteen. Some young people, both white and African American, went on to high school. But few people went to college when Addy was young, and those who did go were usually boys.

Soldier drummer boy.

After teenagers left school, many began working to earn money for their families. Until they married, most continued living at home with their parents. It was hard for black teenagers to find work because many white employers would not hire African Americans. Most young black people who did find work were poorly paid.

During the Civil War, many teenage boys left home to fight. Some soldiers were sixteen or younger when they joined the army. A few were as young as twelve! Girls and their mothers also helped the war effort. They prepared food and clothing for soldiers,

Women and children made personal items for soldiers, like this sewing kit.

60

Over 185,000 African Americans fought in the Union forces.

made flags, and raised money to help sick and wounded soldiers. Almost every American knew someone who was injured or killed in the war. In fact, as many Americans died in the Civil War as in all other American wars before and since combined.

The war changed the lives of all Americans. Many children lost a brother or a father in the war. Some families who lived near an army camp or battleground had their homes and possessions taken away from them.

Children like Addy celebrated the end of the war for many reasons. The end of the war meant the end of slavery, the end of suffering caused by the war, and the hope that families would finally be together again.

When the war was over, soldiers went home to loved ones.